THE JUNGLE BOOK

by RUDYARD KIPLING

#6 The Brave Little Seal

Adapted by Diane Namm

Illustrated by Nathan Hale

STERLING

New York / London

www.sterlingpublishing.com/kids

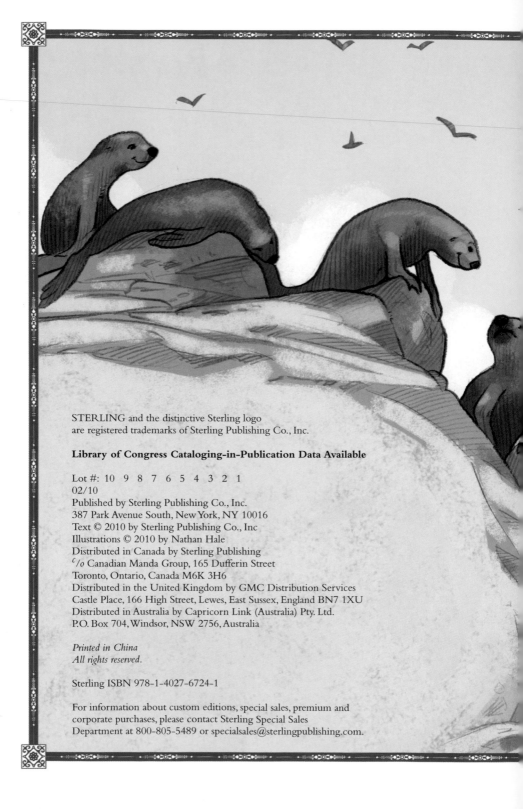

STERLING and the distinctive Sterling logo
are registered trademarks of Sterling Publishing Co., Inc.

Library of Congress Cataloging-in-Publication Data Available

Lot #: 10 9 8 7 6 5 4 3 2 1
02/10
Published by Sterling Publishing Co., Inc.
387 Park Avenue South, New York, NY 10016
Text © 2010 by Sterling Publishing Co., Inc
Illustrations © 2010 by Nathan Hale
Distributed in Canada by Sterling Publishing
^{c}/o Canadian Manda Group, 165 Dufferin Street
Toronto, Ontario, Canada M6K 3H6
Distributed in the United Kingdom by GMC Distribution Services
Castle Place, 166 High Street, Lewes, East Sussex, England BN7 1XU
Distributed in Australia by Capricorn Link (Australia) Pty. Ltd.
P.O. Box 704, Windsor, NSW 2756, Australia

Sterling ISBN 978-1-4027-6724-1

For information about custom editions, special sales, premium and
corporate purchases, please contact Sterling Special Sales
Department at 800-805-5489 or specialsales@sterlingpublishing.com.

Contents

Run Away!

Once upon a time,
there was a place
called Seal Haven,
where all the Arctic seals lived.
One spring, a special
seal pup was born.
His name was Kotick.

From the time he was born,
Kotick knew he was special.
He could not wait to do
everything the grown-up seals did.

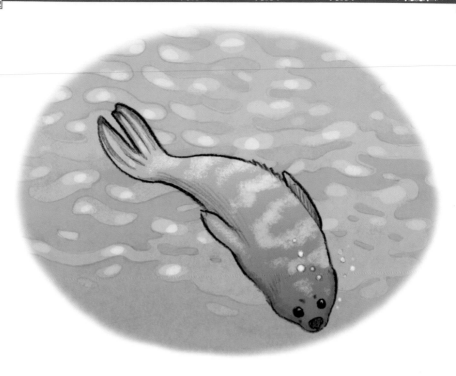

He was the first seal pup
to crawl and swim.
He could dive the
deepest in the sea.
He was the first
to catch a fish.
And he was always
first to the cliff top.

One day, Kotick went
exploring by himself.
That's when he saw
the seal hunters!

"Look! A white seal!" a hunter shouted.

"He's bad luck! Catch him!"

Kotick raced into the sea.

He swam as fast and as far as he could.

Kotick's Search

Kotick swam and swam.
After many miles,
he came up for air
and scrambled onto
an icy bank. There were
no seals in sight.
Kotick saw a crowd of
giant, sleepy walruses.

"Wake up! Wake up!"
shouted Kotick.
"Who are you to talk to me?"
asked the biggest walrus of all.
"The seals need help!"
Kotick explained. "They
need a place safe from the hunters."

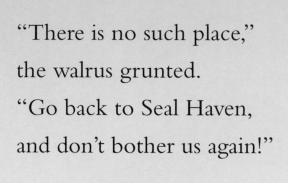

"There is no such place,"
the walrus grunted.
"Go back to Seal Haven,
and don't bother us again!"

Kotick did not know what to do.
"Ask Wise Old Seal
on Old Seal Rock,"
said a seagull as she flew by.

Kotick swam over sharp rocks.
He swam through terrible waves.
He swam until at last he
came to Old Seal Rock.

"Wise Old Seal," Kotick said.
"Where can I find a land
where the seals will be safe?"
Wise Old Seal thought a moment.

"Kotick, you are very special,"
said Wise Old Seal.
"There has never been a white
seal born on our beaches before.
You were sent to us to save
the seals from the hunters.
Find the sea cow. She will
show you where to go."

Kotick slipped back into the sea.

"Where can I find the sea cow?"

Kotick asked the polar bear,

the whale, the shark, and the fish.

"Swim north," they told him.

"Swim as far as you can go."

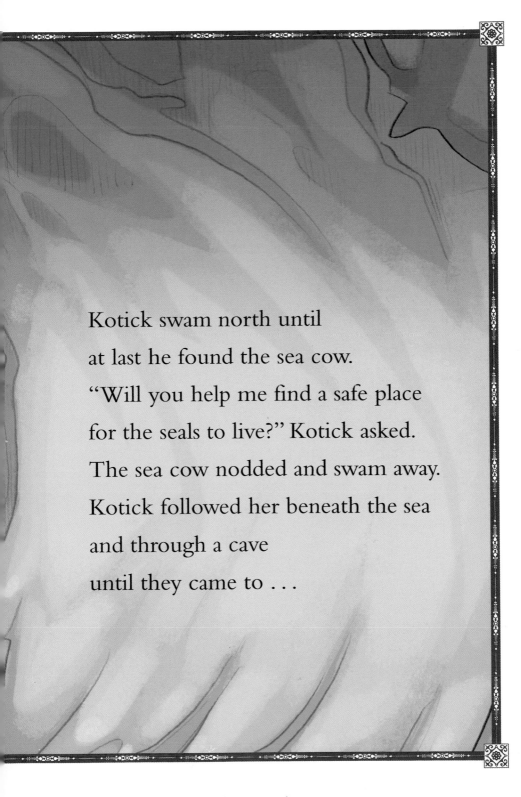

Kotick swam north until
at last he found the sea cow.
"Will you help me find a safe place
for the seals to live?" Kotick asked.
The sea cow nodded and swam away.
Kotick followed her beneath the sea
and through a cave
until they came to . . .

Paradise

. . . a beautiful beach with
nothing but sea cows!
There were smooth rock piles
where baby seals could be born.
There were sandy playgrounds
where young seals could have fun.
And there were warm grassy
spots where the seals could nap.

"There are no hunters here,"
Kotick said.
"This is the perfect place!"
Then Kotick swam all the way back
to Seal Haven to tell the others.

Kotick returned to
Seal Haven as fast
as he could swim.
But hunters were on their
way to Seal Haven too!

Saved!

Danger was getting
closer and closer.
Kotick shouted to warn
the other seals, but they
laughed and ignored him.

Then Wise Old Seal swam up.
"I am the last of the old and wise.
In my early days, there was a story
often told that one day a white seal
would come and lead the seals
to a quiet place.
That day has come.
We must follow Kotick if we hope
to survive."

Just then, the hunters arrived.

"What do we do?" the seals cried.

"Follow me!" Kotick shouted.

Kotick led the seals into the water.

They dived deep beneath the sea.

They swam through the underwater cave,

until they arrived at . . .

. . . every seal's paradise!

"We're safe, now!" Kotick said.

"Thanks to Kotick," shouted one seal.

"Hurray for Kotick!" shouted another

and another until Kotick's

name rang out across the beach.

From that day forward, Kotick was

known as the bravest seal of all.